# Now, Now Brown Cow!

**ReadZone Books Limited**

First published in this edition 2015

© in this edition ReadZone Books Limited 2015
© in text Christine Moorcroft 2010
© in illustrations Tim Archbold 2010

Christine Moorcroft has asserted her right under the Copyright Designs and Patents Act 1988 to be identified as the author of this work.

Tim Archbold has asserted his right under the Copyright Designs and Patents Act 1988 to be identified as the illustrator of this work.

Every attempt has been made by the Publisher to secure appropriate permissions for material reproduced in this book. If there has been any oversight we will be happy to rectify the situation in future editions or reprints. Written submissions should be made to the Publisher.

British Library Cataloguing in Publication Data (CIP) is available for this title.

Printed in Malta by Melita Press.

ISBN 978 1 78322 132 5

**Visit our website: www.readzonebooks.com**

# Now, Now Brown Cow!

Christine Moorcroft
and Tim Archbold

Brown cow says, "Now,
I'm going to town.

I shall powder my nose...

...and put on a gown.

I shall spend this pound
that I found
on the ground."

The owl frowns.

The hound growls.

The little mouse
runs out of the house.

Then the farmer gives
a shout!

# "You are not going out!."

I shall not allow...

...a cow
to go to town.

So now,
cow,
go and lie down."

Brown Cow flounces
into the house
and on to the couch.

"Ouch!" howls the farmer's
wife. "Ouch! Ouch! Ouch!"

# Did you enjoy this book?

## Look out for more *Redstart* titles –
### first rhyming stories for beginning readers

**Alien Tale** by Christine Moorcroft and Cinzia Battistel
ISBN 978 1 78322 135 6

**A Mouse in the House** by Vivian French and Tim Archbold
ISBN 978 1 78322 416 6

**Batty Betty's Spells** by Hilary Robinson and Belinda Worsley
ISBN 978 1 78322 136 3

**Croc by the Rock** by Hilary Robinson and Mike Gordon
ISBN 978 1 78322 143 1

**Now, Now, Brown Cow!** by Christine Moorcroft and Tim Archbold
ISBN 978 1 78322 132 5

**Old Joe Rowan** by Christine Moorcroft and Elisabeth Eudes-Pascal
ISBN 978 1 78322 138 7

**Pear Under the Stairs** by Christine Moorcroft and Lisa Williams
ISBN 978 1 78322 137 0

**Pie in the Sky** by Christine Moorcroft and Fabiano Fiorin
ISBN 978 1 78322 134 9

**Pig in Love** by Vivian French and Tim Archbold
ISBN 978 1 78322 142 4

**Tall Story** by Christine Moorcroft and Neil Boyce
ISBN 978 1 78322 141 7

**The Cat in the Coat** by Vivian French and Alison Bartlett
ISBN 978 1 78322 140 0

**Tuva** by Mick Gowar and Tone Eriksen
ISBN 978 1 78322 139 4